This book
belongs to

....

Puddle's Fan Pages

Here's what other children have to say about their favourite puppy and his first adventure!

"The book is really good! I like Ruby best because she is a little girl like me and very caring about Puddle." Caitlin, age 6

"I liked it a lot and couldn't wait for Mummy to read the next chapter. Can I have a dog like Puddle please?" Madeleine, age 5

"I liked the bit about the princess the best. I love princesses." Lucina, age 5

"We really enjoyed reading this book and thought Puddle was lovely. Our favourite part was when Ruby found Puddle and when they were trying to win the race on the magic carpet ride. Puddle the naughtiest puppy is great!" Zoe, age 7 and Sophie, age 6

"**I REALLY** liked the book! The character I liked the most is Puddle because he can do magic. The best bit was when they had the flying carpet race." Saara, age 6

"Puddle is the best puppy ever. I couldn't wait to read the next page to find out what happened next ... like when Puddle nearly fell off the magic carpet ... I was so excited my tummy was tingly and I couldn't sit still in bed!" Ella, age 7

"I think other people should get this book, it's great." Ava, age 6

Magic Carpet Ride

Other books about
Puddle the Naughtiest Puppy:

Toyshop Trouble

Ballet Show Mischief

Rainforest Hide and Seek

Puddle
the naughtiest puppy

Magic Carpet Ride

by Hayley Daze
illustrated by Ann Kronheimer
cover illustrated by Paul Hardman

A catalogue record for this book is available from the British Library

Published by Ladybird Books Ltd MMX
A Penguin Company
Penguin Books Ltd., 80 Strand, London WC2R 0RL, UK
Penguin Books Australia Ltd., Camberwell, Victoria, Australia
Penguin Group (NZ) 67 Apollo Drive, Rosedale,
North Shore 0632, New Zealand

I

Series created by Working Partners Limited, London WC1X 9HH
Text © Working Partners Ltd MMX

Special thanks to Mo O'Hara

ISBN: 978-1-40930-326-8
Printed in England

Mixed Sources

Product group from well-managed
forests and other controlled sources
www.fsc.org Cert no. SA-COC-001592
© 1996 Forest Stewardship Council

FSC

For Daniel and Charlotte,
my two curious adventurers

When clouds fill the sky and rain starts to fall,
Ruby and Harry are not sad at all.
They know that when puddles appear on the ground,
A magical puppy will soon be around!

Puddle's his name, and he's the one
Who can lead you to worlds of adventure and fun!
He may be quite naughty, but he's clever too,
So come follow Puddle – he's waiting for you!

A present from Puddle:

Look out for the special code at the back of the book to
get extra-special games and loads of free stuff at Puddle's
website! Come and play at www.puddlethepuppy.com

Contents

Chapter One
The Naughty Puppy

Ruby hopscotched down Grandad's garden path, splashing her way through the puddles. Her wellies sent water spraying high into the air. Dots of mud splattered her dress. Ruby loved how the raindrops caught in her plaits.

"The crowd goes wild," Ruby yelled as she hopped, skipped and jumped towards an imaginary finish line. "Ruby, the World Champion Puddle Jumper, wins again!" Ruby raised her arms in victory, but just as she reached the last puddle, a puppy splashed right into the middle of it, soaking her.

"Hello!" Ruby said, smiling and wringing out her plaits. "Where did you come from?" She leaned down to check the puppy's neck for a collar, but he didn't have one. "Are you lost?"

The puppy shook his head. Raindrops flew from his floppy ears.

"Would you like to play with my cousin Harry and me?" Ruby asked.

The puppy raced Ruby up the garden path. They burst through the front door of Grandad's cottage and into the lounge.

Harry was sitting in the window seat, reading his puzzle book. He looked up and pushed back his glasses, which had slipped down his nose. "I don't think puppies

are allowed in the house," he said, looking worried. "Especially not wet puppies with muddy paws!"

The puppy bounced around the room, knocking over Harry's pile of library books and Grandad's umbrella stand. He ran up to Harry and snatched the puzzle book right out of his hands.

"Hey, you give that back," Harry called, but he was grinning. "You're not just muddy, are you? You're a naughty puppy!"

Harry chased the puppy and Ruby chased Harry. Ruby and the puppy left a trail of muddy prints across Grandad's lounge floor, which

was now littered with books and umbrellas.

The puppy came to a sudden stop in the middle of the Persian rug. Harry fell over the puppy, tumbling head over heels, and Ruby fell over Harry. They all lay on the rug in a tangle of arms, legs – and a wagging tail. The puppy wriggled free, dropped the book in front of Harry, and licked him on the cheek. His bright eyes sparkled with mischief.

"Yuck," Harry cried, picking up his puzzle book by the corner. "It's all slobbery."

"Come on, Harry," Ruby begged. "The puppy just wants to play, and so do I. We've been stuck in Grandad's cottage for two whole rainy days. And the rain still hasn't stopped!"

Ruby pointed at the raindrops running down the window panes and the dark clouds in the sky.

But Harry stood up, dusted himself off, and returned to the window seat. He opened his puzzle book and started reading. Harry loved reading more than anything.

Ruby sighed – then smiled when she saw that the puppy was nipping playfully at the tassels on the corner of the rug. Every time he pulled at a tassel, he rolled over on to his back. Ruby knelt down and rubbed his tummy.

"You want to roll up in the rug, don't you?" she said. "So do I!"

Ruby lay down on the rug and rolled over and over so the rug became a tube with just her pigtails hanging out.

"Help! Harry!" Ruby cried in a muffled voice. "The Giant Carpet Monster has got me."

The puppy jumped on top of the rolled-up rug. Ruby could feel his wagging tail bumping against it.

Ruby squealed and wiggled her wellies inside the rug. She squirmed along so she could poke her head out of the end. Her messy pigtails swung back and forth as she tossed her head and shouted, "Save me!"

"That is not a Giant Carpet Monster," Harry said. "That is Grandad's old Persian rug."

Ruby immediately stopped wiggling. "It's make-believe," she said.

"I don't believe in make-believe," Harry said.

"How could you not . . ." Ruby started to say, but the puppy began

to tug on the frayed edge of the rug
with all his might. Ruby rolled free
and landed with a thump against
Grandad's coffee table, toppling the
dish of peppermints and scattering
the contents of Harry's pencil case on
the floor.

"I told you he was a naughty
puppy," Harry said, hopping down
and gathering his collection of pencils

and coloured pens.

"My hero," Ruby said, hugging the puppy a little too tightly. "You saved me!"

The puppy wriggled free and dashed back outside, with Ruby close behind. The rain was falling heavily now. One of the raindrops landed with a plop on the tip of Ruby's nose. Others slid down her cheek, her dress and even the toes of her wellies.

"Come on, Harry," Ruby called. She watched him pull on his wellies and peer into the garden.

"It's too muddy to play outside," Harry said, looking down at his nice white shirt and his pressed beige trousers.

The puppy ran towards Harry, splashing through the puddles, and jumped up to his chest. Harry nearly fell over.

"Urgh!" groaned Harry, wiping mud from his shirt. "I don't think

I've ever been this filthy in my life." But he was smiling happily, and he bent to stroke the puppy's soggy ears.

"I think he likes you," Ruby said. "I wonder what his name is."

"We should call him Puddle," Harry said. "He splashes in enough of them."

"Would you like that name, boy?" asked Ruby.

The puppy offered her a muddy paw.

"That's a deal, then. Puddle it is," Ruby said, shaking his paw. She and the puppy splashed in every puddle on the path, Ruby's pigtails bouncing up and down. "Come on, Harry, try this. It's great!"

Harry wiped specks of muddy water from his glasses. "I don't think so," he said.

Puddle barked and danced circles around a big puddle. Ruby skipped over, splashing water into the air as she went.

The puppy looked from Ruby to Harry.

"Stop him," Harry groaned. "He's going to jump."

But the puppy leapt into the puddle and . . .

Ruby gasped and looked at Harry. His eyes were wide as he stared at the puddle.

"The naughty puppy's disappeared!" they said together.

Chapter Two
Puddle Makes a Splash

The water was still rippling around the spot where Puddle had jumped in. "Where did he go?" Ruby asked, dropping to her hands and knees. All she saw was her reflection, made topsy-turvy in the water. "He's vanished."

"He can't have done," Harry said, scratching his head.

"Well, I'm going in after him."
Ruby stood up tall, straightened her
dress and tugged on her plaits for
luck.

"I don't think that's a good idea –"
Harry began to say.

But Ruby swung her arms back.
"Here I go!"

"Wait for me!" Harry cried.
With a shimmering splash they
jumped, wellies first, into the puddle.

Ruby and Harry landed with a thud on a shabby carpet. For a moment, Ruby thought she was back in Grandad's cottage, playing on his old Persian rug. But then she heard Puddle bark. He wagged his tail and looked happy to see her. Ruby stroked his head.

"Where are we?" Ruby asked.

Puddle barked and jumped over Ruby and Harry, landing right in the lap of a young boy. He was sitting cross-legged at the far end of the carpet, staring wide-eyed at them through the fringe of his dark hair. Harry adjusted his glasses and waved nervously.

"Where did you come from?" the boy asked.

"We're really sorry to drop in on you like this," Ruby said. "I'm Ruby, and this is Harry and that –" she pointed to Puddle – "is Puddle."

The boy laughed and tickled Puddle's chin. "I'm Aziz," he said.

The sun bounced off white-walled buildings and painted roofs. Ruby

could smell delicious spices and orange blossom. "We're definitely not in Grandad's village any more," she said.

Then the carpet began to ripple. The ground seemed to shift below their feet. Puddle raced from one side of the carpet to the other, while Ruby, Harry and Aziz bounced up and down as if the carpet had become a trampoline. Harry lost his balance and, as he tumbled to the edge of the carpet, he looked over.

"Ruby," Harry said with a gulp, "we're not on the ground."

"We're floating!" Ruby squealed with delight. She scooped up Puddle, who licked her face. He seemed to like floating as much as Ruby did.

Aziz laughed at their excitement. "This is my flying carpet," he said. "Hold on, because here we gooooo!"

They zoomed over a bustling market-place filled with flowers, fruit, pottery and brightly coloured rugs. In the distance Ruby could see a palace with a shimmering golden dome.

"It's beautiful," Ruby said. "Look at all the tall towers with the onion-shaped tops."

"Minarets," Harry said. "They're called minarets. I read it in a book once."

Ruby tilted her head and stared
at her brainy cousin. "Minaret.
Sounds like the name of a sweet."
She licked her lips. "A kind of twirly
watermelon-and-grape-flavoured
lollipop."

She heard a whizzing sound
behind them.

"Watch out!" shouted a loud voice.

They felt a bump as something knocked into their carpet and sent it spinning off in another direction.

"What was that?" Ruby cried.

Puddle barked at something nearby. Ruby turned and saw a swarm of flying carpets gathering over the market-place. Carpets of every size and colour circled above the excited crowd.

"Flying carpets! Real flying carpets – hundreds of them!" Ruby shouted. She grabbed Puddle and hugged him tightly. "Isn't this wonderful?"

Chapter Three
The Magical Race

Harry wiped his glasses again and again, as if he couldn't believe his eyes. "It's amazing," he said, "but it's also impossible. Carpets can't fly. There must be engines on them somewhere." He pushed his glasses back into place and tried to peek under the carpets.

"Or it could be magic!" Ruby said

as the sky filled with flying carpets.

"This isn't a real flying carpet, is it?" Harry asked.

"Oh yes, it's real," Aziz said, "and it goes really fast. Hold on!"

As Aziz spoke, the sound of a gong filled the air.

The next moment, all the flying carpets zoomed forward. Ruby grabbed on to Harry, and Puddle grabbed hold of a worn bit of carpet with his teeth.

"It's a magic carpet race!" Ruby shouted. They sped through the air, making Ruby's plaits take flight. Puddle's ears flapped in the wind.

"I don't mind flying, but maybe not

quite as fast as this," Harry said, now lying flat on the carpet like a starfish. Ruby thought he was starting to turn a little green.

Aziz's flying carpet shot past other racers above and below them. The crowd in the market-place cheered.

Aziz steered the carpet left to pass one carpet and then swerved right to overtake another.

Aziz leant forward and the carpet plunged downwards, like a rollercoaster speeding down a hill. Ruby and Harry gripped the tassels of their carpet. Ruby's stomach jumped and danced. She liked the feeling. It made her want to scream and giggle all at once.

But Puddle wasn't holding on any more. The little puppy rolled past Ruby, tumbling over and over.

"Oh, no," Ruby cried. "Puddle can't stop!"

She scrambled towards him but she was too late. Puddle had toppled over the side.

Aziz levelled the carpet and Ruby

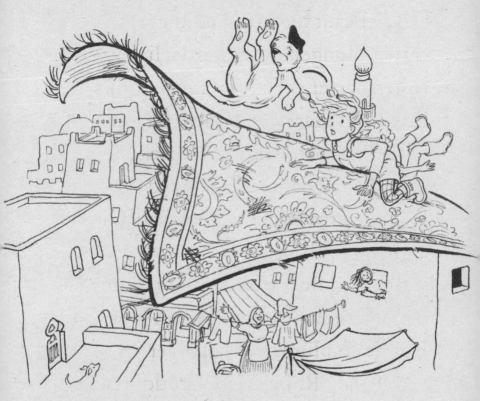

heard a loud yelp.

"Puddle? Is that you?" She looked over the edge.

Puddle was dangling underneath, clinging to a single carpet thread.

Chapter Four
Ruby to the Rescue

"Hang on, Puddle!" Ruby shouted.
She hooked one arm under the puppy's
body and held tightly to the carpet
with the other. Harry grabbed Ruby's
legs to steady her. But Aziz had to

make another sharp turn to avoid a
tall rooftop. Ruby lost her grip and
Puddle flew high into the air.

"Puddle!" Ruby screamed as she
dived to the back of the carpet and
reached over the side. Puddle landed
in her outstretched arms.

"See, I've got you," she whispered to the puppy as she lifted him safely back on to the carpet.

"Is he OK?" Aziz asked, pushing his hair back off his face.

"Woof! Woof!" Puddle wagged his tail. They all laughed. Aziz turned his attention back to the swarm of flying carpets.

"This is some race," Harry said to Aziz. "What do you get if you win?" Ruby saw that Harry now looked slightly less green.

"The winner will be granted one wish by Princess Amber," Aziz said, but never took his eyes off the flying carpets ahead of him.

"Are you going to wish for a new flying carpet?" Ruby asked, poking her finger through one of the carpet's many holes.

Aziz darted past another racer. "My family's carpet is very old, but still very fast," he said.

"I can see that," Harry said. "So what would you wish for?"

"I must keep it a secret for now," Aziz said, rounding another corner, "or it might not come true."

Puddle barked loudly as a thick red carpet, ridden by a girl in a turquoise robe, overtook them.

"Oh, no, you don't," Aziz said. "Hang on. Here we go again!"

By now they knew to hold on tight as Aziz picked up speed. He was soon gaining on the other carpet.

"Aziz, watch out for those minarets ahead," said Harry, his voice shaky again.

Aziz grinned. "That's exactly where I'm heading!"

Puddle hid his face beneath his paws.

Chapter Five
A Close Finish

Aziz swung his carpet round so it was racing straight towards the towers.

"My carpet's smaller than that girl's thick red carpet," he shouted. "I can go between the minarets, but she'll have to go around them."

Ruby stroked Puddle's ears, and the puppy uncovered first one eye and then the other. The carpet hurtled towards the minarets. Puddle barked and nipped at the edge of the carpet. He pulled it in towards Ruby, Harry and Aziz.

"Puddle's right," Aziz called. "Quick, pull in the sides; it's going to be close."

Ruby and Puddle grabbed one side and Harry quickly tugged on the other. Their carpet raced smoothly right between the minarets!

"You certainly know how to fly a carpet, Aziz!" Ruby said. She looked at the other flying carpets they would have to pass to win the race. Aziz was definitely the youngest racer.

"I can't find a gap that I can get through!" Aziz called to Ruby and Harry. "We'll have to slow down."

As Ruby and Harry searched the skyline for a carpet-sized space, Puddle barked loudly. He pointed his whole body, nose first, towards a patch of blue sky.

"Well done, Puddle," shouted Ruby.

"It's going to be tricky," Aziz said, flicking the hair from his eyes. "I'm not sure I can steer the carpet through there."

"We can help," Harry said. "If we put all our weight on one side, it'll make the carpet turn better. I read about it in my physics book."

"Just like surfing," Ruby said and scrambled to her feet, balancing on the carpet. "Let's do it!"

"Well, actually, surfing uses water, not air," Harry corrected her. "But it's the same idea, I suppose. Now, everybody lean right!"

Ruby, Puddle and Harry all leaned right. Puddle was clinging to Harry, and Harry was clinging to Ruby. The carpet started to tip, and Aziz sped

past two of the other racers.

"Now left!" Harry yelled.

They rolled to the opposite side, Puddle grabbing the hem of Ruby's dress with his teeth. Aziz zoomed past three more racers, and the carpet slid through the gap that Puddle had pointed out. The tassels of Aziz's carpet nearly brushed the other carpets as they passed.

"That was close," Ruby said. "I can see the finish line, there on the roof of the palace!"

"It's not over yet," Aziz said. "There's still one more racer ahead of me, and he's really fast."

Aziz sped up and soon the two carpets were racing neck and neck, neither one able to take the lead. They were only a few carpet lengths from

the finish.

"How can we go faster?" Ruby wondered.

Puddle hopped from Ruby's lap and rolled along the carpet. Ruby reached for the puppy, but Puddle barked and backed out of her reach. He shook his head from side to side and rolled over again. He grabbed the edge of the carpet in his teeth and began to roll himself inside it.

"Puddle," Harry groaned. "You'll fall off again."

But Ruby realized what the puppy was doing. "That's it!" she shouted. "If the carpet was shaped like a rocket, long and thin . . ."

"That's a great idea," Aziz shouted. "You're a genius, Puddle!"

He steered the carpet left and then quickly rolled it right, spinning them round and round. The carpet rolled into a tube with the friends tucked inside.

"Woooaaaah!" shouted Ruby and Harry together as the carpet raced forward, rocketing towards the finish line.

Chapter Six
The Princess's Problem

The rolled-up carpet zoomed over
the finish line by a nose – Puddle's.
Ruby, Harry, Puddle and Aziz all
spilled out on to the palace roof,
laughing as the magic carpet unrolled
itself.

"You did it!" Ruby cheered.

"We all did it," Aziz said.

Then the gong sounded again and a

willowy young girl stepped out of the golden dome on the palace roof. She walked slowly towards the winning team, her long yellow dress and orange silk veil blowing in the wind.

"That's Princess Amber," Aziz whispered to his new friends. He stepped forward and bowed.

Ruby and Harry copied Aziz. Puddle lowered his head too.

"Please rise," Princess Amber said. "I must congratulate you on winning."

"*Shokran*, Princess – much thanks," Aziz said. "I am Aziz and these are my . . ." He paused. "My co-pilots, Ruby and Harry." Puddle barked.

"Oh, and who could forget Puddle?"

"*Salaam*, Princess," said Harry.
Princess Amber nodded.

"What did you say?" Ruby
whispered to Harry.

"It's 'hello' in Arabic," Harry said.

"I took a few Arabic lessons last year before I started French."

Puddle bowed and the princess reached down to stroke him.

"You all raced with courage," Princess Amber said, "and you truly deserve the prize." She looked away.

The princess's eyes were cloudy and sad.

"Excuse me, Your Highness, but is something wrong?" Ruby asked.

Princess Amber sighed. "It's my magic lamp," she said.

"So many things are magic around here!" Ruby said. "Lamps, carpets … Do you have magic toasters as well?"

Ruby was pleased to see Princess Amber give a small smile. Then the princess held up a golden lamp. "It is an old oil lamp that I was given for my birthday," she said. "Inside it is a magic genie who grants wishes." Her smile faded. "But he won't come out."

"Wow, there's a genie in there?" Ruby stared at the lamp.

"And the genie will grant Aziz his wish?" Harry asked.

"Yes," the princess replied, "if you are able to remove him from the lamp." She gently placed it on the ground in front of them.

Puddle barked at it crossly.

"Puddle," Ruby said, "the genie won't come out if you're rude to him."

Puddle licked the lamp and rubbed against it.

"Whooo, hoo, haaa, haaa," a voice echoed from deep within the lamp, which began to shake from side to side. "No, stop, please! Haaa, haaa! It tickles – stop!"

Puddle shot behind Harry's legs and peeked out at the quivering lamp.

"Maybe there's some secret button that opens it?" Harry said, pressing a square marking on the top. Then he wiggled the handle, turned the whole lamp upside down, and pressed the

circles underneath and the diamond shapes on the sides.

"Uuurp!" burbled the lamp as a wisp of greenish smoke came out of the spout. "Please stop. You're making me lamp-sick."

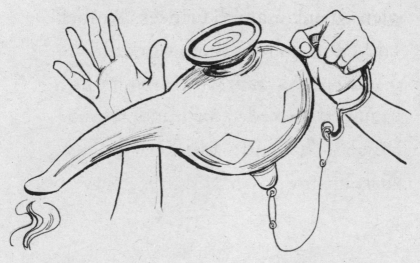

"Sorry," Harry said. He gently turned the lamp so it was the right side up again.

"It's hopeless," sighed the princess.

"Wait!" said Ruby, taking the lamp from Harry. "It's a magic lamp, right? Maybe there's a magic word."

"I've tried all the magic words I know – Abracadabra, Alakazam and even Open Sesame," Princess Amber said. "But none of them worked."

Now it was Aziz who hung his head and looked sad. "I understand, Princess," he said. "I will not get my wish."

Chapter Seven
Granting Aziz's Wish

"There must be something we can do," Ruby said, pacing back and forth across the palace roof.

Puddle was scampering about on the patterned tiles, chasing his tail and barking. He bumped into a refreshment table, sending oranges and cakes rolling across the floor.

"Puddle, you naughty puppy,"

Harry said. "Keep still and let us think, please."

"That's it!" Ruby exclaimed. She picked up the lamp and raised it over her head. "The most magical word of all is . . . please."

White smoke poured from the lamp's spout.

It twirled into the shape of a large, round genie. The genie floated above the lamp, still connected to it by a swirl of smoke.

"You did it," said Princess Amber, her eyes shining with happiness. "Thank you!"

Ruby stared at the genie. "Wow, you're much bigger than I thought you'd be," she said.

"Are you saying I'm fat?" asked the genie. "Look, there's not much room to exercise in that lamp."

"Sorry," said Ruby nervously. "You look great. Very magical and swirly."

"You think so?" the genie said. "You don't think all the smoke is too much?"

Puddle barked and shook his head.

"Dear Genie," Princess Amber said, "now that you are here, will you please grant our wish?"

"Why do people always jump straight to the wishing?" the genie asked, shaking his head. "Not even a cup of tea or a how-do-you-do. A genie can get very thirsty in that tiny lamp."

Ruby could see Princess Amber pull her orange veil round to cover a smile. "My apologies, Genie," the princess said. "But Aziz has won the magic carpet race and your first wish belongs to him."

"Winning a race isn't so special," the genie said with a frown. "I could fly pretty fast when I was a young genie." He zoomed left then right, up then down, leaving a criss-crossing trail of smoke behind him.

"What a grumpy genie," Ruby whispered to Harry.

"I heard that," the genie said, landing next to Ruby. "I don't feel like granting any wishes today."

Puddle began to growl. He even nipped at the trail of smoke the genie left behind.

"Puddle's right," Ruby said, wagging her finger at the genie. "You aren't being very nice."

"I think granting wishes must be fun," Harry said. "You get to make people happy."

"Yes," Ruby agreed. "What an amazing power to have!"

The genie puffed out his chest and beamed at them. "I suppose you're right," he said. "Let the wishing begin."

Puddle trotted across the roof to a marble staircase. "Woof! Woof!"

Princess Amber turned to the friends. "Everyone is waiting to meet you," she said, picking up the lamp, with the genie floating above it. "Will you join me for the wish-granting ceremony?"

They descended the marble stairs, which led down from the palace roof on to a stage decked in brightly coloured banners. The cheers of a huge crowd filled the air.

Princess Amber stepped forward. "May I present the winner of the magic carpet race – Aziz!"

Aziz's magic carpet floated on to the

stage with a sparkling silver trophy resting on top. The princess took the trophy off and handed it to him.

"Aziz, please tell me – what is your wish?" Princess Amber asked.

Aziz brushed his hair from his face. "I wish for a new house that is big enough for my whole family to live in together," he said.

The genie was bowing and waving to the crowd. When Ruby gave him a nudge, he clapped his smoky hands together and Aziz's family magically appeared on the stage – his mother, father, brothers, sisters, aunts, uncles, cousins and even his cat.

The genie whispered to Aziz, "I suppose you want your own room, too?"

Aziz smiled and nodded.

"Your wish is granted," the genie boomed, pointing into the distance. An arrow of smoke whizzed to the hillside and exploded, creating a huge heart-shaped cloud.

The smoke cleared to reveal an enormous white house with blue doors and lilac flowers trailing up the walls.

It was perfect!

"That's for us?" Aziz gasped.

The genie laughed. "It certainly is."

The applause of the crowd filled the air. The sound was louder than any thunderstorm Ruby had ever heard.

"I'm so happy that you got your

wish," Ruby shouted over the noise.
Puddle gave a happy bark as if he
agreed.

"I couldn't have done it without all
of you," Aziz shouted back.

Harry tugged on Ruby's sleeve. "There's just one problem."

"What could be wrong with today?" Ruby asked. "We've won a magic carpet race, met a princess and a genie, and Aziz and his family have a new home. What more could anyone wish for?"

"Aziz has his new home," Harry said, twisting his shirt-tail in his hands. "But we don't know how to get back to Grandad's cottage!"

Ruby realized that Harry was right. How would they ever get home?

Chapter Eight
Puddle's Magic

Puddle barked and began to race in circles round and round Ruby and Harry.

"What is that silly puppy doing?" Harry asked.

Ruby felt her stomach go all fizzy, like the bubbles in lemonade. "Look!" she said. "The world's gone all fuzzy."

"It's like looking through a rain shower," Harry said.

The faces of Aziz and his family, Princess Amber and the genie became a blur as the puppy ran even faster.

Ruby grabbed Harry's hand. "I think Puddle is taking us home," she cried.

She and Harry both called
"Goodbye!" to their new friends, and
could just hear them shout farewell
in return. Ruby's skin tingled and
her plaits began to spin. Then she
closed her eyes against the whirlwind
Puddle was creating.

When Ruby opened her eyes again,
she saw the most beautiful sight in
the world, even more beautiful than
the minarets – it was Grandad's
cottage. She and Harry were standing
among the puddles on Grandad's
garden path.

  "That was . . . unbelievable,"
Harry said, smoothing his hair and

straightening his glasses.

"But where's Puddle?" Ruby asked, searching for the puppy.

"He's disappeared again," Harry said. He peered into the puddles. "Maybe he wasn't real. Maybe none of it was."

Ruby stared round the soggy garden. The rain had almost stopped, and she had to squint as the sun peeked through the clouds. There was a flash of movement as something darted out from behind a tree.

"Puddle!" Ruby cried happily, and she ran after the little puppy. "I thought we'd lost you. Come on – let's go inside for tea."

Ruby and Harry walked up the path.

"Keep up, Puddle!" Ruby called. But the little puppy had gone. In his place, lying on the damp grass, was an ancient oil lamp. Ruby picked it up.

"It's just like Princess Amber's magic lamp," she said, drying it on the hem of her dress.

"We'll never forget our adventure now," Harry said. "I hope we see Puddle again soon."

"Maybe he'll come back next time it rains," Ruby said. She gazed out for one last time over the garden. The naughty puppy was nowhere to be seen.

"Goodbye, Puddle," she called out softly. "Come to see us again soon!"

Can't wait to find out
what Puddle will do next?
Then read on! Here is the first
chapter from Puddle's second
adventure, Toyshop Trouble...

Toyshop Trouble

"Look at all these toys!" Ruby
gasped. She and her cousin Harry
were in Grandad's lounge, peering
inside an old toy chest. Ruby
could see a jumble of model trains
and aeroplanes, marbles and
motorcars. They were the toys
Grandad had played with when
he was a little boy.

"What do you think that is?" Harry asked, pushing his glasses up the bridge of his nose and pointing to a gleaming red-and-green object.

"Let's have a look," Ruby said, leaning so far into the toy chest that only her feet were sticking out. She moved aside a big wooden truck, a tank, and some small metal cars that got tangled in her long plaits. Then she grabbed the green-and-red toy and passed it to Harry.

"It's a clockwork train," Harry said, his eyes shining. At the front of the train was the engine, and there were three carriages behind it.

"It's the 2:15 from Paddington,"

Ruby said, "and Teddy is going to visit Chips!" Teddy was Ruby's toy duck-billed platypus. He had a long, furry brown body, four big feet and a beak like a duck's. Stitched to his bottom was a new pink tail Ruby's mother had sewn on after a tug-of-war accident.

Ruby sat Teddy on one of the carriages and Harry turned the key in the top of the train and set it on the carpet. It chugged across the room in the direction of Chips, Harry's toy robot.

"Go, Teddy!" Ruby said.

Tappety, tappety, tap. The train ran into a desk leg and ground to a halt, but the noise of drumming carried on.

Tappety, tappety, tap.

Ruby leapt up in excitement. "It's raining!" she cried, running to look at the raindrops pitter-pattering against the windows. Ruby could feel bubbles of excitement fizzing up inside her. The last time it rained, a little puppy called Puddle had arrived, and they had all been swept away on a magical adventure!

The back door blew open, hitting the kitchen worktop with a bang. A bundle of fur zoomed into the room like a rocket, knocked over the clockwork train, Chips and Teddy, and leapt into the toy box. It landed

— *plumpf* — on the toys inside.

"Puddle!" Ruby shouted, clapping her hands with delight.

She and Harry looked inside the toy box to see a little puppy staring back at them. His pink tongue was lolling out and his white tail wagged happily.

Harry patted Puddle on the head. "I'd forgotten what a naughty puppy he is."

"He's pretending to be a toy!" Ruby said, laughing. She scooped him up in her arms. "He's definitely as cuddly as Teddy."

"Woof! Woof!" barked Puddle, as if he agreed. Then he wriggled free, dashed across the room, through the kitchen, and into the rainy garden.

"Come on!" Ruby shouted with excitement. They rushed after him.

Outside, Puddle bounded down the garden path, splashing in the puddles. His tail was wagging so hard that a blur of raindrops sprayed out. Ruby held out her hands to catch some of the sparkling drops. From behind his glasses, Harry's eyes were shining. Puddle stopped in front of a particularly large pool of water and raced round and round it. The raindrops were making the surface ripple and shimmer. He crouched down, then jumped into the water with a splash – and disappeared right through the puddle. Just like last time.

Ruby grinned at Harry. "Are you ready for our next adventure?" she asked.

"What if the magic doesn't work today?" Harry asked. "The likelihood of another magic puddle is very low."

"We won't know until we try," Ruby said. "One, two, three – JUMP!"

***

To find out what happens next, get your copy of TOYSHOP TROUBLE today!

Toyshop Trouble

Join Puddle, Ruby and Harry
on their next exciting adventure!

This time Puddle's
magic takes them
to an amazing
toyshop. Professor
Toyjoy needs help
to win the big toy
competition!
Will Puddle be
able to save the day?

Find out in TOYSHOP TROUBLE...

Ballet Show Mischief

Go on a beautiful ballet adventure
with Puddle, Ruby and Harry.

The children are
whisked away to a
wonderful ballet
show, but the shy
ballerina has stage
fright. The show
must go on! Will
Puddle be able to
find a solution?

Find out in BALLET SHOW MISCHIEF ...

Puddle
the naughtiest puppy

Rainforest
Hide and Seek

Have you ever wanted to see a rainforest?

Puddle uses his
magic to take Ruby
and Harry through
a puddle and into an
incredible animal
adventure. Things
keep going missing
in the rainforest
– can Puddle find
out why?

Find out in RAINFOREST HIDE AND SEEK . . .

Dragon Dance

Join Puddle, Ruby and Harry on
their new adventure in Chinatown!

Li wants to make
his grandad proud
by appearing in the
Chinese festival.
Can Puddle and the
children help him
to get Lucky the
dragon to dance?

Find out in DRAGON DANCE…

Puddle
the naughtiest puppy

Magic Mayhem

Ruby and Harry are amazed to find themselves in a medieval castle …

… when Puddle takes them on their latest adventure! They meet a magician's apprentice who is in deep trouble. He's lost his spell book. Can Puddle save the day?

Find out in MAGIC MAYHEM …

Dogs Trust

Hi, it's Ruby and Harry here with Puddle the puppy! We hope you've enjoyed our magical journey as much as we have!

We now want to share something else with you and tell you all about an amazing organisation called **Dogs Trust**.

Dogs Trust looks after lots and lots of real dogs and puppies – in fact, they are the largest dog charity in the UK (ask your parents or teacher what a charity is!). They will be joining us in every one of our books to tell us about a real dog's needs and teach us how to take care of dogs.

Always remember, Puddle is a magical dog, while real dogs and puppies are living animals who need a lot of care, love and attention.

About Dogs Trust:

- Dogs Trust is the UK's largest dog charity and would like all dogs to be able to enjoy a happy life in a loving home.
- Sadly, some dogs are not very happy or healthy, so Dogs Trust works hard to help them get better and find new homes.
- Dogs Trust helps adults and children learn about their dogs and what is good for them.
- Dogs Trust has 18 homes for dogs. These are places where they eat, sleep and have fun!
- In 2009 Dogs Trust cared for nearly 16,000 dogs. Can you imagine that many dogs?

Congratulations – now you know about **Dogs Trust!** Why not tell all your friends about what you have learnt today?

See you next time, when we will be learning all about being safe around dogs.

Remember, "A dog is for life, not just for Christmas®" Dogs Trust has 18 Rehoming Centres around the UK and Ireland. To find out more please go to:
 www.dogstrust.org.uk

For more fun and games please go to:
www.learnwithdogs.co.uk

Pieces of Puddle!

Look carefully at the picture of Ruby and Puddle opposite. It has several pieces missing! Can you work out which of the jigsaw pieces on this page fits into each space?

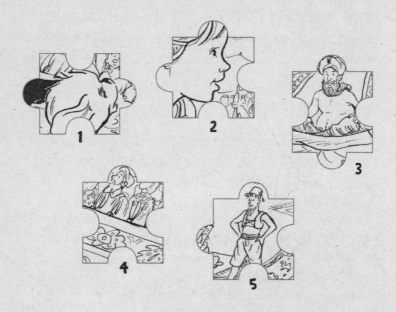

Shadow Puppies!

Study this cute picture of Puddle.
Then work out which of the shadows
on the opposite page would exactly
match the picture.

A

B

C

D

Answers on the next page

Answers to puzzles:
Pieces of Puddle: 1-D, 2-C, 3-B, 4-E, 5-A
Shadow Puppies: A

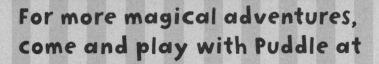

For more magical adventures,
come and play with Puddle at

www.puddlethepuppy.com

Use this special code to get
extra special games and free
stuff at puddlethepuppy.com

LAMP